LOOK OUT FOR THE WHOLE SERIES!

**Hodder
Children's
Books**

A division of Hachette Children's Books

Special thanks to Lucy Courtenay and Artful Doodlers

Chapter One

It was a bright, breezy morning. The Famous Five –
Jo, her dog Timmy and her three cousins Allie, Max
and Dylan – headed out of Jo's house. They had
skateboards tucked under their arms.

Jo was in her usual tomboy gear: dungarees,
hoodie and muddy boots. Allie, on the other hand,
had gone for a pink outfit with matching top,
tights, skirt, shoes and bag.

Max fancied himself as the best skateboarder
among his cousins. He thrust back his shoulders
and took a deep breath of fresh sea air. They
were only a mile from the coast here. "Today seems
like a day ripe for kickflips," he grinned. "Kickflips

and heelflips." He dropped his board on the veranda and demonstrated. To the untrained eye, the two flips looked more or less the same. But in skateboarding, there was a whole world of difference.

"I beg to differ," interrupted Max's dark-haired cousin Dylan. "It strikes me as nosegrind weather." Straightening his glasses, he checked out the handrail on the steps that led from the veranda down to the garden. A nosegrind needed something to slide down. The handrail was perfect.

"Wait a minute!" Allie squealed. Dylan almost dropped his board. "Don't anybody move!"

Her cousins waited, agog, as Allie dashed back into the house. When she returned a minute later clutching a necklace, everyone groaned.

"I nearly forgot my 'Hip Kitty' medallion," Allie panted, fixing it round her neck. "It matches my skateboard."

That was Allie all over. Accessorise, accessorise, accessorise.

"You're such a girlie-girl, Allie," Jo sighed. She eyed Allie's little skirt. "And you can't do any moves in a skirt like that. It'll blow up like a parachute."

"I can do any move you can," Allie said at once. "And I'll look great whilst doing it."

She went straight into a magnificent skating routine, kickflipping and heelflipping and nosegrinding perfectly down the handrail. Her cheerleader smile didn't waver from start to finish.

"Woahh!" Allie squealed as she soared off the end of the handrail. "Ah!"

Max laughed. Allie was always full of surprises.

"There you have it, sport lovers!" said Dylan, speaking into an imaginary microphone in the style of a sports commentator. "The gauntlet has been thrown down, the challenge undertaken. Who will emerge victorious?"

Max assumed the stance of a valiant knight heading off to battle. "To the half-pipe!" he roared.

Laughing and joking, the cousins rounded the corner to where they had built a skateboarding half-pipe from an old metal drainage pipe. Max, Dylan and Timmy settled down at the edges while Jo and Allie took up their positions on the platforms at opposite ends of the half-pipe.

"I wish I'd had time to sell tickets to this," Dylan murmured wistfully as Jo and Allie padded up and fixed on their helmets. He put on his commentator voice again. "The ultimate female cousin skateboarding contest – Beauty and the Beast!"

Jo stopped tightening the chinstrap on her helmet and glared at Dylan. "Hey!" she complained.

Dylan raised his hands. "I don't mean it, Jo," he said hastily. "But you've got to admit – it's a grabber."

At a nod from Jo, both girls rolled from their platforms into the metal half-pipe and immediately swooped up to the other side. They turned round and skated back down into the pipe, gaining momentum, then soared into the air in a pair of matching somersaults.

As they reached the apex of their somersaults, the half-pipe glowed a strange, sparkly orange. Before the Five's startled eyes, it rapidly disintegrated into a pile of crumbling rust. It was as though a swarm of metal-eating termites had demolished it.

"Woaahhh!" Jo and Allie yelled, flailing in mid-air as their landing pad vanished. Jo came down in a patch of mud. Allie's skirt fluttered and filled with air, gently dropping Allie on a drier patch of ground.

4

"Hey, it did blow up like a parachute!" said Allie, looking pleased as she brushed herself down. "That was lucky."

Rubbing mud from her face, Jo frowned. Then she asked the question they all wanted the answer to. "What happened to the half-pipe?"

Chapter Two

The half-pipe's wooden launching platforms were still intact. The cousins gathered beside one of the platforms in a semi-circle, staring at the muddy patch that moments before had been the big metal half-pipe.

"Yeuchh," Jo grumbled, getting to her feet. "A metal half-pipe can't just disappear . . ."

"It *didn't* just disappear," said Jo's mum George from somewhere behind them.

The Five turned. George was approaching from the house, side by side with a pony-tailed, denim-clad guy in his fifties.

Briskly, George brushed the mud off Jo and

6

Allie's clothes while the pony-tailed guy munched on the contents of a take-away food container he was carrying.

"Both in one piece," George said. "Splendid. Technically, your skate thingy was *eaten*." She smiled cheerfully, adding: "Chomp, chomp, chomp."

Pony-Tail scraped some more food from his take-away box. "That's right, little dudes," he said in an American accent. He held up a small vial of some kind of gloopy orange substance. "It was gobbled up by my formula, which I call 'The Gimble Formula'," he said proudly. " 'cos it's a formula, and I'm a Gimble."

George introduced her companion to the Five. "Professor Howard Gimble," she explained. "We knew each other at university."

Howard Gimble held up two fingers. "Peace," he said. He waved his container at the kids. "Want some of this potato salad and pickled onions? It's righteous. I know, 'cos it's all I ever eat."

"I helped Howard isolate the enzyme that makes his metal-devouring gel work," George said enthusiastically. "It's from ragwort!"

Jo's mother was a botanist, famous for

7

her greenhouses and her exotic plant-collecting experiments as well as for a youth spent solving crime.

"That's pretty amazing gel," Max said, impressed. "But are there *that* many half-pipes that need to be got rid of?"

Howard Gimble shrugged apologetically. "Sorry, dude-ling. We thought it was just an old drainage pipe."

"Howard hopes to use his gel to get rid of all the rusty old scrap metal littering the world," George explained.

The Five stared at the tiny vial. It was incredible to think that it had just turned a huge metal pipe into a pile of rust shavings.

"That gel must be awfully valuable," Max said at last. "Aren't you afraid someone – let's say, aliens or the government – might try to steal it?" Aliens and conspiracy theories were big with Max.

Howard Gimble shook his head. "Dude-ling – negative vibe," he said. "I'm a passenger on Spaceship Earth – next stop, world harmony."

The professor scraped at his take-away box one last time. Then he upended it and gave it a shake.

"Harsh – out of pickled onions," he groaned. "Make that 'next stop, the fridge'. Then my nap."

Giving his peace sign again, the professor started back to the greenhouses. Never one to miss an opportunity to make money, Dylan hastened after him.

"Mr Gimble!" the others heard him calling as he ran after the professor. "I can help market this! You could call it 'Dissolve-O!' or 'The E-Rust-icator'!"

Leaving Dylan to it, the others headed for the back door to the house.

"Since his gel doesn't eat mud, could you hose off my shoes, Allie?" Jo asked, stopping at the outside tap.

Timmy picked up the hose in his teeth and handed it to Allie. As Allie turned it on and began squirting water at Jo's feet, a handsome sixteen-year-old emerged from the kitchen door. He was studying a notepad in his hand and frowning. Looking up, he caught sight of Howard Gimble and Dylan heading back to the house. "Professor Gimble!" he shouted, in a deep American drawl. "I called the local dump. They'll let us test the gel on the old cars there." He gave the professor a

9

smiling thumbs-up. "Our first step toward a more beautiful world!"

"Righteous," Professor Gimble nodded.

Allie turned to see who owned the new voice. The hose in her hand squirted Jo full in the face.

"Hey!" Jo spluttered. She wiped the water from her face, smearing mud across her cheeks. As she did so, she caught sight of the boy on the back veranda. Her eyes widened. Then, astonishingly, she turned bright red.

"Kids, this is Gavin, Professor Gimble's research assistant," George introduced them airily. She hadn't noticed Jo's strange reaction. "Gavin – the Kirrin clan – ooh, minus Dylan."

"Jo, I'm Jo, my name's Jo, I'm Jo," Jo squeaked a little breathlessly. She cleared her throat. "Jo," she added, in case Gavin hadn't heard her the first four times.

"Gavin – I've got errands to run in town," George said as Allie looked at her cousin oddly. "I can drop you at the dump a little later."

"Or I could take Gavin there now," Jo blurted. She looked at Gavin. "The dump's lovely at this time of year," she said earnestly.

Gavin smiled. It tugged cutely at the corner of his mouth. "That's OK, bro," he said. "I need to consult with Professor Gimble first."

Giving a little wave, Gavin headed back inside, followed by George and Max.

Jo was smiling foolishly at the spot where Gavin had been standing.

"Here comes the bride," Allie teased, *"da-dum-dee-dum . . ."*

"If that means you think I like him, yes – I like him," Jo said. She bristled a bit. "So?"

"So he called you 'bro'," Allie pointed out. "He thinks you're a *guy*. That's not good. I can help you with your look if you want."

Jo bristled a little more. At this rate she was going to turn into a hedgehog. "I can look after my 'look' myself, thank you very much," she snapped, and turned on her heel to go inside the house.

Allie chewed her lip, looking worried. *"Here comes the bride,"* she sang thoughtfully to herself, heading inside the house after Jo. "All dressed in . . . dungarees and dirty boots. Eeeg . . ."

Chapter Three

A little later that day, Gavin was out on the veranda, making entries in his notebook. Other notebooks, plus a small calculator, lay on the table beside him. An open jar of Professor Gimble's metal-melting formula sat beside the calculator. Making the most of the shade beneath the table, Timmy was gnawing loudly on a bone.

Allie, Max and Dylan came out of the house with a tray of tea: scones, butter, jam and a jug of iced tea. They set it on the table beside the jar of gel.

"Gavin, right?" Dylan asked, helping himself to a scone. "Dylan." He smiled winningly. "About this gel," he began. "I've got some great names. 'Metal Melt'. 'Scrap-B-Gone'. 'Eat My Rust'."

"Well, those are all very interesting," Gavin said, looking up. "But I think it's more important that Max doesn't eat the gel."

Everyone turned to look at Max, who was holding a scone. He had taken a spoon and dipped it into the gel by mistake. As he moved the spoon towards his scone, the gel started to eat the spoon. Max was left holding just the handle and looking startled.

"Oops – that wasn't jam," he said, frowning. "That's powerful stuff."

Gavin carefully put the lid on the gel. "And people all over the world want to get their hands on it," he said, tightening it and pushing the jar away from the tea tray. "That's why the professor came here – so we could hide out and test it in peace."

"Sorry I'm late – I hope I haven't missed tea!" Jo chirped.

She stepped out of the doorway to join them. There was a clattering sound as Timmy dropped his bone. Dylan spat out a mouthful of iced tea. His tomboy cousin was wearing a hideous purple satin bridesmaid's dress, complete with puffy sleeves and a wide hoop skirt.

As Jo stepped forward, Allie swooped in, grabbed her by the arm and towed her swiftly back inside.

"What are you *wearing*?!" Allie hissed, after checking that Gavin was out of earshot.

"I decided to wear a dress," Jo said defensively. She smoothed out a purple wrinkle. "There's nothing wrong with it."

"Not if you're auditioning for *HMS Pinafore*," Allie muttered, shaking her head.

"I was a bridesmaid for my cousin Kala," Jo said, waving an irritable hand at her cousin. "It's my only pretty dress – it's fine."

She swept back outside again, knocking over a garden gnome with her hoop skirt.

"That's quite a dress, Jo," Gavin said admiringly.

Jo shot a triumphant look at Allie, who had come scurrying out after her.

Gavin smiled. "Going to a costume party?"

This wasn't quite the response Jo had hoped for. "Um, yes," she said, covering frantically. "The

Falcongate . . . Fancy Faire . . . for Frilly Females. I'm a frilly female!"

She tried a little twirl, but stopped halfway when her attention was caught by something on the tea table. "Hey, a bug —"

Swiftly, Jo picked up a spoon and whacked a scone. "Got it," she said, sounding pleased, before flicking the insect off and popping the scone in her mouth. "Good scone," she said with her mouth full. She slapped Gavin heartily on the back. "So," she said. "You ready to go to the dump?"

Gavin shook his head regretfully. "Still waiting for the professor—"

BOOM!

The sound of a huge explosion rocked the veranda. The jug of tea toppled over, the scones hit the floor, and Timmy hit the scones for a quick snack. Everyone else looked shocked.

"What the heck was *that?*" Gavin gasped.

Dropping everything, the Five raced off across the lawn. Jo gathered armfuls of purple satin, trying to keep up with the others. It was a novel experience. She was usually the one leading the field.

Over the treetops at the end of the garden, they could see an enormous geyser of water spraying up to the sky.

"That looks like it's on Mr Woolsey's farm," Dylan shouted to the others.

They pelted on. Another geyser sprayed up, joining the first. This time, the roly-poly figure of a farmer appeared, bobbing helplessly on top of it.

"And *that* looks like Mr Woolsey!" Max shouted back.

"We're on our way, Mr Woolsey!" Allie called, speeding up. "Don't go anywhere!"

"Where's he going to go?" Dylan asked.

Nobody answered. They all swerved out of the garden gate, down the lane and across the way to Mr Woolsey's farm.

Several other jets now joined in the fun. A number of Mr Woolsey's sheep looked up from where they were cropping the rich grass in the field beside the farm buildings. They didn't seem very excited at the sight of the farmer flailing around on top of a jet of water.

"Woah-wooaah-wooooaahh!" howled Mr Woolsey, whooshing up, then down, then up again.

The kids and Timmy raced up to the farmer's geyser.

"My Aunt Louise is a plumber," Max shouted up to the helpless farmer, shading his eyes from the sun. Mr Woolsey looked like a tweed-clad ping-pong ball from where they were. "She takes me on jobs with her sometimes. I'll see if I can shut off the water."

As Max went off in search of the mains water tap, Dylan grabbed a nearby bucket and a large rock. He turned the bucket upside-down and plopped it smartly over the geyser. Then he sat on the bucket, clutching the rock to weigh himself down. The water stopped immediately. Dylan looked pleased with himself. Then he looked up.

Nothing was keeping Mr Woolsey in the air any more.

"That might not have been the best move . . ." Dylan began.

He got no further. Mr Woolsey fell out of the sky and landed on top of him.

Chapter Four

"Wooahhh – ooofff," grunted Mr Woolsey, landing hard.

"Ohhhh," Dylan groaned in a muffled voice from somewhere underneath the farmer's tweed bottom.

Mr Woolsey looked around for the source of the voice. He stood up. Dylan was lying spread-eagled and squished deep in the mud.

"Ah, there you are," Mr Woolsey said, his brow clearing as he looked down at Dylan. "Thank you, my boy."

"That's OK," Dylan mumbled through a mouthful of mud.

Max had found the mains valve up near a barn. "Can't . . . move . . . it," he groaned, heaving and tugging at the rusty wheel. With a squeal, the wheel began to turn. "Moving . . . it," Max added, with an extra heave.

The round valve spun off its pipe and started rolling away.

"Losing it!" said Max in dismay. He started to run after the valve. "Hey, come back . . . ! This never happened to Aunt Louise . . ."

As Mr Woolsey recovered his breath, Timmy ran across the farmyard towards a low wooden building. He barked sharply at the door, glancing back at the others.

"That's the barn for my lambs – it's filling with water!" Mr Woolsey said in dismay.

Dylan tried to open the door. It wouldn't budge.

"The water's holding the doors shut," he said, standing back after a couple more useless efforts. "Anyone got a wrecking ball?"

It was an ambitious request. Allie was already using her ingenuity, and had started climbing a ladder up to the low barn roof. Jo followed.

RRRIP!

There was a tearing sound as Jo's purple satin skirt caught on one of the ladder rungs and tore.

"I can sew that," Jo said, hardly glancing back over her shoulder as she climbed. There wasn't a minute to lose. The lambs in the barn were in grave danger.

RRRIP!

"I can sew that," Jo repeated, gritting her teeth as she pulled free from another ladder rung.

RRRRIPPP!!

"Or I can just tear it off," Jo said, and gave her skirt a rough tug as she heaved herself on to the roof.

The purple skirt tore away completely, revealing the hooped petticoat underneath. Ignoring the problem, Jo scrambled up beside Allie and peered down through a skylight.

Down below, the lambs were happily doggy-paddling round the barn. Jo prised the skylight open, dipped her arm in and withdrew it, holding a lamb by the scruff of its woolly neck. She passed it to Allie, before putting her arm back in to retrieve another.

"Ah, you're lucky we got you out of there," Allie said, cuddling the lamb. It baaed and batted its long eyelashes at her. "Wool shrinks. You'd be like a little tiny tennis ball."

Allie leaned over and gently dropped the lamb down from the roof to where Timmy was waiting. The lamb landed on Timmy's back. Without turning a hair, Timmy reached around and took the lamb in his mouth, lifting it carefully to the ground.

Still muddy from head to toe, Dylan was working on the barn door hinges. From his position on Mr Woolsey's shoulders, he was now loosening a hinge some way up. The hinge ripped off. A torrent of water gushed out of the barn. Dylan and Mr Woolsey were both sent flying.

"Wooahh!" Dylan shouted, shooting backwards in a gush of cold water. "Well, I needed a bath . . ."

A lamb jumped happily on to Dylan's chest and started licking his face and giving little baas. Dylan started laughing. The lamb's tongue tickled.

Then all at once, the geysers stopped pumping water.

Max jogged over, looking pleased with himself. "The main valve worked, but the pressure regulator on this one was gone," he said, indicating the round valve by the barn that had broken off in his hand. "Someone must have taken it."

"That would be deliberate sabotage," Jo said.

Dylan noticed a glimmer in the mud near the broken valve. He pounced, and held up something shiny and grapefruit-sized. "A tin-foil ball," he said, turning it round in his hands and examining it. "Al Fresco Freddy saves tin-foil and makes these things."

Al Fresco Freddy was Falcongate's best-known character. He lived in an old hovel in the woods, and was known for collecting weird things and generally behaving like a clown after too many cream cakes.

"Why would Freddy take a pressure regulator?" Allie asked.

"He's a loon," Dylan said helpfully. "Maybe it was a Christmas gift for his gran."

"Jo and I'll go into the village and talk to him," Allie decided. "You guys go home and see if Gavin needs help with his experiments."

"Good," Jo said as the guys jogged off back to the house. She looked ruefully down at her muddy, ripped dress. "I don't want Gavin to see me like this anyway. He already thinks I'm a bit weird."

Mr Woolsey was still waving gratefully as Dylan and Max turned in through Jo's garden gate.

"I've got some more brand names," Dylan confided to his cousin as they jogged up the path. "'Brass-Tastic'. 'The Alu-minimizer'. 'Gold-B-Gone'..." Dylan paused at that one. "Wait," he said, "why would you get rid of gold? People love gold. Focus, Dylan!"

Timmy barked and picked up speed. He raced ahead of the others, leaping on to the veranda.

Looking woozy, Gavin was handcuffed to the railings. There was a cut on his forehead, a blindfold over his eyes and tape plastering his mouth shut.

Dylan and Max quickly tore off the blindfold.

"Gavin, what happened?" Max asked urgently as Gavin slipped free from the handcuffs.

Gavin reached up and ripped the tape off his mouth. "Professor Gimble's been kidnapped!" he gasped.

In the dreadful silence that followed, Dylan

imagined he could hear the professor crying for help – somewhere . . .

"Hello? Help! Anybody? I'm the victim of a very harsh incident – bummer!"

Chapter Five

Max, Dylan and Gavin dashed into the house. They gazed around the empty guest room in horror. It looked as if a stampede of buffalo had made their way through the middle of it.

"I was working on the veranda," Gavin said helplessly. "I heard the professor shouting for help, and then somebody banged me on the head."

Max and Dylan set to work at once, looking for clues. Their experience told them there were *always* clues.

Dylan stopped and examined the floor. "These scuff marks on the floor near the bed are heading that way . . ."

He pointed at the window. Max went over and studied one of the glass panes. "Looks like he cracked the window in the struggle," he said, indicating a small hairline crack in one of the panes.

Dylan picked up the bedside clock. "This clock's broken, too – it stopped at 2:18," he said, showing the clock face to the others. "That's when we were at Mr Woolsey's farm."

"Look at this fabric." Max pulled a small scrap of fabric off the window latch and waved it at the others. "Red and white stripes."

Dylan frowned. "Al Fresco Freddy wears that really old jazz band uniform jacket. That's red and white stripes."

Gavin looked stunned at the number of clues Max and Dylan had already found. "Who's Al Fresco Freddy?" he said, rubbing his head.

"Kind of the local crackpot," Max explained. He put the scrap of fabric carefully in his pocket. "We thought he sabotaged our neighbour's water system as some kind of prank."

Dylan waved the alarm clock. "But he might have done it to lure us away so he could grab the professor," he said grimly.

"That would be pretty serious behaviour for Freddy," said Max, shaking his head. Freddy was weird, but he wasn't dangerous.

Was he?

Max's eyes widened. He'd just remembered something.

"And the girls have gone to town to look for him . . . !"

Unaware of the drama back at the house, Jo and Allie walked along the pavement in Falcongate. If Jo felt a bit stupid in the tattered remains of her hooped dress, she didn't show it.

"So where do you want to start looking for Freddy?" she asked, peering down a couple of dark alleys as they passed.

"In here," said Allie. She dragged Jo smartly through a shop doorway.

"Whaaaa . . ." Jo protested. She blinked in the bright shop light and looked around. They were in a ladies' fashion boutique. "I don't think Freddy hangs out in dress shops," she said with a frown.

"We'll find Freddy later," said Allie. She was already rifling through the racks of clothes. "Right now, we're finding you a new look."

"But we need to look for Freddy," Jo began.

Allie fixed her with one of her special Allie gazes.

"Well . . . all right," Jo sighed. She glanced down at her wrecked and muddy outfit. "I tried *my* way of being girlie and Gavin looked at me like I was a zit."

Allie beamed with relief. "Great – I finally get to make you over!" she cried, clapping her hands. "This is better than Christmas! Let's see – where should we start . . . ?"

Soon, the floor of the boutique was littered with outfits. The shop assistant looked a bit dazed, but hurried back and forth with armfuls of clothes for Jo to try on. Allie examined everything with an eagle eye. Half of it was sent back before Jo even got to try it on.

Jo came out of the changing room in a fake leopard skin hat and cats-eye sunglasses. "Well, we *shouldn't* start here," she growled.

"It's the movie-star look!" Allie assured her, prowling round and examining her cousin from every angle. "A lot of guys go for it. Say something star-like."

Jo thrust her hand out. "I don't talk to reporters," she snarled. "Get that camera out of my face or I will smash it."

There was a pause.

"Let's try something else," Allie said brightly.

The next ensemble had Jo wearing a psychedelic bandana on her head, heart-shaped granny glasses and love-beads.

"You're a flower-child!" Allie announced, doing a willowy, hippy-style dance. "A blossom grooving on the vibe of the universe!"

Jo did her best to copy Allie. But her dance was more clunk than funk.

"That's more a blossom who's mad at the vibe of the universe," Allie said, stopping.

The pile of rejects was growing higher. Next, Jo came out wearing a floppy hat, dark glasses and a grim expression.

"You're a femme fatale!" Allie said hopefully. "Say something mysterious and intriguing."

Jo thought. "You know how when you clean a sink and all the hair's stuck together by some gunk?" she said at last. "What *is* that stuff?"

Allie scratched her head. "Too bad Professor

Gimble didn't invent a formula for girlie-ness," she sighed.

Meanwhile, out along the coast, a rusty old ship moored to an ancient buoy was shaking and heaving violently. Inside, Howard Gimble was wrestling with his bonds.

As the professor wriggled, a grizzled old sailor clumped into the cabin in heavy rubber boots. He had a wild white beard and a cloud of white hair crammed underneath a bright yellow sou'wester.

"Ready to give me that formula for the gel?" growled the old salt.

"Never," Professor Gimble panted. "I'm going to use that formula to save the planet."

"A waste!" said the old sailor in disgust. "I'll use it to get rich as an admiral! If places like Falcongate don't pay me not to, I'll destroy everything made of metal . . ."

The villainous old man drifted off. His eyes went dreamy. Professor Gimble knew he was imagining a host of horrors. Wrecking Falcongate's bronze statue of Sir Francis Drake, for example. Destroying the prison bars in the Falcongate police station and allowing prisoners to escape . . .

"You'll never get the formula out of me," the professor cried.

The old salt laughed nastily. "I'll get it," he said. "When you get hungry enough."

He swung round on his rubber boots and stomped out of the cabin.

"This is not cool, man!" Professor Gimble shouted after him furiously. He struggled again. "*Not* cool!"

Chapter Six

Allie rushed out of the boutique, looking very excited. "OK, world!" she cried dramatically to a group of passers-by. "Meet the new Jo!"

Cautiously, Jo stepped outside. She was dressed almost exactly like Allie. A flowing scarf was draped around her neck. Long beads clanked on her chest. A fringed belt hung around her waist, and she had a pair of high heels on her feet.

"The new Jo looks a lot like the old Allie," said Jo, looking down at herself. "But I can work with it." She took a step. Her high heels tripped her up. "Ohh – except for these heels," Jo growled, struggling to get her balance. "These things are *so* uncomfortable."

Timmy trotted down the street towards them. When he saw Jo, he broke into a run. Leaping up, he licked Jo's face all over.

"Timmy!" Jo spluttered, wobbling madly. Jumping dogs and high heels really didn't go together. "What are you doing here?"

"He has a note on his collar . . ." said Allie, noticing.

Jo unfolded the note. *"Meet us at the bus stop as soon*

as you get this. Professor Gimble has been kidnapped. PS – tell Allie to charge the battery on her phone," she read.

Allie looked shocked. She pulled her phone out of her pocket. "Oh, it *is* dead," she wailed. "No wonder I haven't gotten any text messages in the last five minutes."

Timmy barked, encouraging Allie and Jo to follow him. Minutes later, they saw Max and Dylan waiting on a bench near the centre of Falcongate.

Max and Dylan watched as Allie rushed and Jo lurched towards them.

"You notice anything different about Jo?" Dylan said with a frown. There was something he couldn't put his finger on.

"Whaaa!" Jo shouted, falling flat on her face. She struggled up, only to fall over a few paces further on.

Max scratched his head. "She seems to be falling down a lot," he suggested.

"Whaaa!"

Needless to say, Allie reached her cousins first.

"Someone's grabbed Professor Gimble – we're afraid it was Freddy," Dylan explained, as Jo struggled grimly to her feet for the third time.

"We think the sabotage at Woolsey's farm was a

diversion," Max put in.

"So," Jo panted as she reached the others at last, "we really *have* to find Freddy."

Allie glanced across the street. "I think I may have found him . . ." she said.

Al Fresco Freddy was standing in the doorway of Falcongate's pet shop. The shop was run by mild-mannered Mr Weatherwax. It wasn't difficult to scare Mr Weatherwax. Usually, all you had to do was go into his shop.

"You're imprisoning these animals without asking their permission!" Freddy was shouting. Mr Weatherwax looked terrified.

The kids jogged over the road, to see what was going on.

"Animals are meant to roam wild!" Freddy was getting into his stride now. "They're born to bound majestically over mountains, plains and jungle!"

"But I sell bunnies and birdies . . ." Mr Weatherwax said feebly.

Freddy advanced into the shop. "Roam through Falcongate, my friends!" he roared, and started flinging the cage doors open.

A host of pets rushed out into the street as Al

Fresco Freddy marched round the shop freeing everything he could see. When he reached the iguana cage, Freddy stopped and stared. "You, my friend, have wild eyes," he crooned through the bars.

Dylan was nearly knocked over by a flock of escaping parrots as the Five rushed in to help Mr Weatherwax. "Hey – get off – leave me alone!" he shouted, flailing his arms in a cloud of feathers. "Ooopphh . . ."

Timmy barked in delight at the sight of two escaping cats. The cats leaped on to Max's head in terror, hissing and clawing. Max yelped with pain. "Owwww – oooh . . ."

"Aw, bunnies!" Allie said in delight as several rabbits hopped cautiously over the threshold and into the street. "C'mere, cute bunnies!"

But picking up rabbits whilst wearing high heels brings unexpected challenges. Allie fell over before her hands sank into the soft bunny fur. Her legs had got tangled up with each other. "Woahh – ughh," she gasped, and sat down hard on the pavement. "The bunnies are winning!"

A distraught Weatherwax appeared in the door.

"Oh, don't let them get away – they might get rained on!" he wailed.

Dylan produced a top hat from somewhere. He held it out and ran after the bunnies. Obediently, the rabbits hopped into it. Timmy had given up chasing the cats and had now turned his attention to rescuing a kitten and a macaw. Max had the bright idea of tempting the birds by covering himself with birdseed and standing on the pavement. A multicoloured mass of parakeets fell on him, and he walked – a little unsteadily – back into the shop.

Jo chased a pot-bellied pig up the pavement. Her heels were wobbling all over the place. Then her scarf got caught on a tree branch, spinning her round like a top as it unwound. Jo seized the branch and snapped it off. She tied her scarf to the branch's various prongs, turning it into an efficient pot-bellied pig net.

"Got you!" she said, catching the pig and falling over once more. "Whaah!"

The pig nuzzled her apologetically. Somehow, it made Jo feel a little better.

Chapter Seven

When all the animals had been rescued, the Five helped Mr Weatherwax put them all back in their cages. Al Fresco Freddy was still making eyes at the iguana in the corner. The iguana looked a little fed up at having missed his chance of freedom.

"Thank you, children," Mr Weatherwax said. Tears of gratitude started in his eyes. "As a reward, you each get . . . a free cuttlefish bone."

"Good," said Max breezily, taking his bone. "Mine's almost finished."

Ting-a-ling. The shop door opened, and Mr Weatherwax leaped out of his skin as a large lady police officer bustled up to the counter.

"Someone call for Stubblefield?" demanded Constable Lily Stubblefield.

Without needing to be told, Constable Stubblefield strode across the shop towards Freddy. Freddy and the lizard were still staring at each other. When the iguana moved its eyes in odd directions, Freddy copied it in delight.

"Don't annoy the lizard, Freddy," Constable Stubblefield said cheerfully. "Let's get going – you know where the police station is."

Al Fresco Freddy beamed. "I certainly do!" he said, and allowed the constable to seize him.

Mr Weatherwax shrank back behind his cash register as Freddy and the police officer passed his counter. It would take a lot of bunny grooming to calm him down after this little incident.

"Wait a minute, Constable Stubblefield," Jo called, hurrying after the police officer as best she could in her heels. "We need to talk to Freddy."

Stubblefield squinted at Jo in her new outfit. "How come you're dressed like a girl?" she asked suspiciously.

"I'm trying something different," Jo explained.

Constable Stubblefield raised her eyebrows.

"I'll say," she remarked. "If you want to talk to Freddy, you can find him at his new home. Falcongate police cells."

And before the Five could protest any further, the police officer had marched Freddy out of the shop.

Professor Gimble's stomach was growling. He would have given anything for a mountain of pickled onions and potato salad to appear. There would have been the small problem of how to eat it with his hands tied behind his back. But at least he'd be able to smell it.

The door banged open.

"You must be as hungry as a humpback whale," growled the old sailor. He waved a take-away box at the professor. "Give me the formula, and you get pickled onions and potato salad. Mmmmmm . . ."

"You win, dude," Howard Gimble croaked. "Pickled onions get me every time . . ."

Looking pleased, the old salt placed a pad of paper and a pen in Howard's lap. He untied the professor's right hand. "Now write down the formula," he ordered.

Professor Gimble raised his eyes to the rusty, riveted ceiling of his prison. "Forgive me, Falcongate," he groaned, and began scrawling out equations.

Constable Stubblefield had already marched Freddy across the street and shut him in a cell by the time the Five ran after her. Jo was still struggling with her footwear.

"Ah, home, sweet home," Freddy sighed, settling down on the hard bench in his cell. "What's for supper?"

"Pea soup and ham sandwiches," Constable Stubblefield answered. "Should be here any minute."

It struck the Kirrins that Constable Stubblefield and Freddy looked like they'd done this before – on more than one occasion. The police officer's next words confirmed their suspicions.

"Freddy keeps getting himself arrested so he can get free meals," Constable Stubblefield told them, setttling heavily down behind her desk and reaching for an incident report form.

"Was he here at lunchtime today?" Jo asked.

The police officer nodded vigorously. "He was. Stole a bunch of helium balloons and a folding chair. Said he was going to fly across the Channel."

Dylan swung round to the others. "So there's no way Freddy could have planned and executed the professor's disappearance!" he said.

Allie frowned. "Why, because he has a cast-iron alibi?"

"Well, yes!" Dylan paused. "And because he's a complete loon."

Chapter Eight

No one could really argue with this. Professor Gimble's kidnap had been planned by a master criminal – that much was clear. Criminal as Freddy was, he was no master.

Freddy beamed as the police station door banged open. The Five swung round. A smiling man in a striped grocer's apron came in, carrying bags of take-away food.

"Hope we're hungry," said the grocer cheerfully, waving the bags at Constable Stubblefield.

Food and romance novels were Constable Stubblefield's chief passions. Solving crime came a little further down the list. She started up from her desk, reaching for the food bags. As she pushed past Jo, the keys on her belt caught on Jo's dangling bead necklace.

"Arggghh . . ." Jo gargled, grabbing at her necklace and narrowly avoiding strangulation. Irritably she unhooked the beads and threw them in the wastepaper basket. "I didn't know being girlie was so dangerous."

The police officer was happily helping the grocer unpack the food and line it up on her desk.

"Here's the soup," said the grocer, depositing a steaming green tub on top of Constable Stubblefield's incident report form. "Here's the sandwiches and here's a portion of potato salad . . ."

This last container was tiny. Constable Stubblefield looked horror-struck. "That's not a portion," she complained. "That's a thimbleful."

The grocer shrugged apologetically. "All I could scrape together," he said. "Somebody came in earlier and bought all me potato salad."

"Potato salad?" Max said with a gasp. "Professor Gimble said that's all he ever eats."

The Five stared at each other in excitement. Was this their next clue?

"Did he by any chance buy pickled onions as well?" Allie asked.

The grocer looked surprised. He scratched his head. "Every last one," he replied.

"Can you give us a description?" Max said eagerly.

The cousins waited with bated breath. Soon they would know the identity of the kidnapper!

"Sure," the grocer obliged. "Small, round, white, I soak 'em in a special spicy brine . . ."

"Not the onions," Max put in hastily. "The man who bought them."

The grocer's face cleared. "Oh!" he said. He frowned, trying to remember. "Old. Wild white hair. Oilskin sou'wester," he said at last, and shrugged. "Nothing out of the ordinary."

The cousins were confused. The description matched nobody they could think of. Who was behind all this?

As Constable Stubblefield took a forkful of potato salad – and that's all there was really, a forkful – Jo snatched it from her. "Sorry Constable," she said, offering it to Timmy. "Timmy needs to sniff this."

The police officer looked distressed as half of the potato salad slid off the spoon and hit the floor. Timmy took a sniff. He barked sharply, and ran towards the door. It was all the encouragement the others needed. Jo handed the fork back to Constable Stubblefield, and she and the others took off after Timmy.

Constable Stubblefield eyed what was left of her potato salad rather grumpily. Her mood wasn't improved when Al Fresco Freddy leaned up against the bars of his cell and whined: "I want spotted dick for dessert!"

Chapter Nine

Timmy knew where he was going. The cousins dashed after him as he raced through the streets of Falcongate, diving down alleys. They twisted and turned, making their way down to the docks.

Jo was getting better on her high heels. But not much. It took another half an hour and several large bruises to reach the end of an old, little-used pier that jutted out into the sea. The cousins studied the pier carefully as Timmy ran up and down, barking himself into a frenzy.

"This must be where the old fisherman gave up the chase and leapt to his doom in the briny," said Max sombrely.

"Or he might have rowed out to the wreck of that old schooner," Dylan offered, pointing out to sea.

In the distance, they could all see a skiff tied to the hulk of a rusty, abandoned ship that lay drifting just off the coast. The wreck looked almost a hundred years old. Two bare masts thrust into the sky like bony fingers. There was one tattered sail left on the main mast, but most of the rigging hung loose. The hull was made of riveted iron, and the rest of wood. It was a miracle that the ship was still in one piece.

"Anybody got a boat on them?" Jo asked jokingly.

They gazed up and down the pier. Not one single boat had been moored anywhere near.

Then they spotted a pile of wooden pallets tied up nearby. Beside the pallets lay a bundle of rubber inner tubes for tyres, some rope, some netting and a bunch of lifejackets drying on some pilings. They beamed at each other in relief. There was nothing the cousins liked more than building rafts.

"I think we can manage," Max grinned.

An hour later, the kids paddled quietly over the

water towards the rusting ship. They had built a magnificent raft from the inner tubes, ropes and pallets, and were wearing the life jackets just in case their raft wasn't as magnificent as it looked. Within ten minutes, they were rowing up alongside the schooner. The boat loomed menacingly above them as they tethered the raft to one of the tyres hanging over the hull. Max grabbed hold of a slimy old rope ladder that was hanging down from the deck. Silently, they swarmed upwards. Jo pushed Timmy's bottom up with one hand, struggling to prevent her shoes dropping off her feet and plopping into the churning sea below.

They reached the deck and glanced around. There was no one in sight, and the only sound was the moaning and groaning of the old ship beneath their feet as it was battered by the waves.

"Max and I'll start for'ard," Jo whispered, clinging on to Timmy's collar. "You guys start aft."

"Great!" said Allie, starting off with Dylan. She stopped. "What's 'aft'?"

"That's the back of the ship," Jo explained.

"Perfect!" Allie smiled. "And we'll hope the professor's somewhere in between."

Down below, Professor Gimble was wearily writing down the last part of his equation. "There," he said, pushing the pad towards the sailor. "The formula's done."

The villainous old salt looked delighted. He untied the professor's other hand and gave him a plate of potato salad and pickled onions. Gimble fell on the food as though he hadn't eaten all day.

"Pleasure doing business with you, matey," grinned the sailor. He tucked the formula into a pocket on his oilskins. "Hope you can swim. I've spread this all over the ship's hull." Gleefully, he held up a spray-bottle containing the orange gel.

Professor Gimble started up in horror.

"This old rust heap is being eaten like a shark eats a guppy," the sailor crowed.

The iron door of the cabin disintegrated behind them. The Five barged in via the portholes and the skylight in the ceiling. Before the shocked old sailor had time to react, they had surrounded him.

"You're not going anywhere, sailor," said Max. "We cut your boat loose." He pointed at the little spray bottle in the old salt's hand. "And that gel doesn't belong to you."

"Well," the sailor snarled, "then *you* have it . . ."

He sprayed the gel. The orange goop splashed over the Five and the bulkheads behind them. Large areas of the ship's hull began to glow orange, before dissolving away. Dylan lost the metal button and zipper on his jeans, and his trousers fell down. Jo's jewellery sparkled and exploded into dust.

"Saves me the trouble of throwing it away," Jo said, making a grab for the sailor as he tried to get past them.

"Aaaargh!" Max screamed, looking down in horror at the goo on his T-shirt. "I might melt!"

Dylan looked at Max in confusion.

"My mother makes me eat a lot of iron," Max gibbered.

"Aarggh!" roared the old salt. He dodged past Jo. A hole in the side of the ship opened, and water poured in. Thinking to make a break for it through the opening, the sailor dashed for the gap. He was nimble for such an old man. But before he could slip out, Jo grabbed a pulley on a rope and swung it hard in his direction. The hook on the end of the pulley caught in the sailor's white hair – and tore it off completely. The hair underneath was dark and carefully tousled. It was Gavin.

Chapter Ten

Jo leaned back on the ship's hull in shock. She snatched her hand away just as the bit she was leaning on crumbled away. "Gavin?!" she gasped.

Gavin rumpled his hair defiantly. He tore off his beard and gave his chin a good scratch. "That's right," he snarled. "I saw my chance to get rich and I took it."

"And you framed poor Freddy!" Max said indignantly.

Gavin shrugged like he didn't care. "I heard he was the village crazy. I needed to aim suspicion somewhere."

Jo's face went red with fury. "You mean I got all

girlied up for a . . . a cheap crook?" she shouted.

Gavin waved a finger at her. "Not cheap," he said. He took the formula from his pocket and waved it at her. "Soon I'll be a *rich* crook. I'll send you a postcard from Millionaireville!"

Leaping to his feet, Gavin scurried up a staircase to the main deck. The Five shot after him in hot pursuit.

"Ahh, little dudes?" Howard Gimble called hopefully up the now-dissolved steps. "Yo? Still down here . . ."

Water was really flooding through the rusted hull now. The professor's open-toed sandals were totally submerged.

From the deck above, Dylan looked back. He grabbed a metal chain and fastened it to a solid-looking cleat. Then he dropped the end down to the professor below.

The chain wasn't as solid as it looked. Nor was the cleat. As the metal-munching gel made short work of the iron, it dissolved in Professor Gimble's hands. He dropped down, back to where he started.

"Woaaahh," he shouted as he stumbled,

struggling to stay on his feet. "OK, I'll just wait here . . ."

Meanwhile, Max and Jo were still chasing after Gavin. The floors of the metal deck were disintegrating all over. They were forced to jump, leap and grab at some of the loose rigging that was hanging down from the masts, swinging like a pair of Tarzans towards the back of the ship.

"Aah, ahhhh, ahhh," Jo bellowed, swinging wildly. Max did the same.

Gavin stumbled on, diving and landing and dodging the falling parts of the collapsing ship

Allie and Dylan caught up with Gavin on the other side of an open cargo hatch in the deck. Gavin dived down the hatch to the deck below. Having charted Gavin's progress through a number of holes in the deck, Jo and Max now let go of their ropes. They charged up to some tall ventilators on the deck with Allie and Dylan and leaped inside, sliding down into a cabin on the lower deck.

They dropped in a neat semi-circle around the professor's treacherous assistant.

"Two things," Dylan snarled, as Gavin started at the sight of them all. "First, you're not allowed to use any of the names I came up with for the gel. Second – you're nicked."

Jo folded her arms. "Yes," she said in satisfaction. "Even a rat like you can't get off this sinking ship."

Gavin whirled round and sprayed the hull behind him. A hole opened up in the ship wall, revealing the Five's inner-tube raft bobbing on the water outside.

"Since I'm stealing things, hope you don't mind if I take your raft," Gavin grinned, leaping through the hole and landing squarely on the raft. He seized the oars and started rowing steadily away from the doomed ship.

"I wore these heels just for you, Gavin!" Jo shouted in fury, tearing her shoes off. "You might as well have them!"

She hurled one of her shoes straight at the raft. The sharp point of the shoe's heel punctured one of the inner tubes. With a yell of dismay, Gavin began to sink.

"Woahhhhh!"

At this point, a fishing net dropped down from the ship, covering Gavin completely. Max and Dylan started winching him up.

Allie patted Jo on the back. "I *knew* you'd get the hang of high heels," she said proudly.

Back at the docks a little later, the Five and Howard Gimble gathered triumphantly round Gavin, who was still twisting about in the net. Jo reached into the net and plucked out the paper with the formula written on it.

"I'll take this," she said. Gavin groaned and put his head in his hands. "We don't want you having the formula."

"Be mellow," Professsor Gimble grinned. "It's just the molecular structure of potato salad."

"Potato salad?" Dylan repeated.

The professor looked alert. He glanced around. "Where?" he said hungrily. "You got some?"

There was a wail of sirens. Constable Stubblefield screeched to the end of the pier in her police car. A reporter from the *Falcongate Daily Mirror* followed close behind, a camera in his hand.

"Is this the scoundrel who monopolized all the potato salad?" she shouted, striding up to Gavin. Gavin cringed back inside his net.

"Take him away, Constable Stubblefield," Jo said

with relish as the reporter snapped their picture. "I don't think we'll be throwing *this* one back."

Epilogue

Although the Five had come a little too close to the sea during this latest adventure, it didn't stop them from visiting the beach the next day. They had another Handy Hint to film.

Jo operated the videocamera. She aimed it at Max and Allie, who were both sitting in a small rowing boat just offshore.

"Sticky Situation Number Ninety-One," Jo introduced. "You've Got A Hole In Your Boat."

Max raised his voice so Jo could hear him over the waves. "If you're out in a boat, and it springs a small leak, you can use a bit of garden hose to create an automatic bilge pump."

Like a magician's assistant, Allie handed Max a length of rubber hose.

"As long as the hole isn't bigger than the hose, you just force the hose end on to the hole," Max continued.

He demonstrated by pressing the end of the hosepipe over a small hole in the bottom of the boat, which was welling up with water. The water obediently started flowing through the hose and out the other end, instead of soaking Max's trainers. Max pointed it overboard.

"That's all there is to it," said Max, shifting round to face the camera a little better. "The water goes right back into the sea. Ta-da!"

Max made a grand gesture, accidentally moving the nozzle of the hose so it was pointing straight at Allie. There was a gush of seawater and a wail from Allie.

"Just be careful where you point it," said Max, putting down the hose rather hurriedly as Allie jumped on him.

After a brief wrestling match, Max and Allie both fell overboard. As they swam the few metres back to shore, their boat sank slowly beneath the waves.

So much for *that* Handy Hint.

Read the adventures of George and the
original Famous Five in